A Hmong Cinderella

Jouanah

Adapted by

Jewell Reinhart Coburn with Tzexa Cherta Lee

Illustrated by

Anne Sibley O'Brien

 Shen's Books

To my parents, Ralph and Jewell Harkness Reinhart Sr.,
who so lovingly touched me with their magic wand
of vision, compassion, and possibility.
J.R.C.

To my people and my family.
T.C.L.

For my parents, John and Jean Sibley,
whose love & pioneering spirit have opened worlds for me,
including that of the Hmong.
A.S.O.

English text copyright © 1996 by Jewell Reinhart Coburn with Tzexa Cherta Lee.
Illustrations copyright © 1996 by Anne Sibley O'Brien.
Spanish and Hmong text copyright © 1996 by Shen's Books.
Spanish translation by Clarita Kohen.
Hmong translation by Jean Moua and Tzexa Cherta Lee.
All rights reserved.
This book, or parts thereof, may not be reproduced in any form
without permission in writing from the publisher.
Shen's Books, Walnut Creek, CA
Book design by Greta D. Sibley.
Decorative patterns by Norman Sibley.
Printed in China

First Edition
10 9 8

Library of Congress Cataloging in Publication Data

Coburn, Jewell Reinhart.   Jouanah: a Hmong Cinderella /
adapted by Jewell Reinhart Coburn with Tzexa Cherta Lee;
illustrated by Anne Sibley O'Brien.
[32] p. 26 cm.
Summary: Despite a cruel stepmother's schemes, Jouanah, a young Hmong girl, finds true
love and happiness with the aid of her dead mother's spirit and a pair of special shoes.
English   ISBN   1-885008-01-5
Spanish   ISBN   1-885008-02-3
Hmong   ISBN   1-885008-03-1
1. Hmong (Asian people) — Folklore.   [1. Fairy tales.
2. Hmong (Asian people) — Folklore. 3. Folklore — Laos.]
I. Lee, Tzexa Cherta. II. O'Brien, Anne Sibley, ill. III. Title.
PZ8.C64Jo 1995   398.22'089'95 — dc20   95-36353   CIP   AC

Publisher's Note

This centuries-old folktale was introduced to us by Blong Xiong in a story entitled "The Poor Girl." Another version of the story, "Ngao Nao and Shee Na," can be found in *Folk Stories of the Hmong* by Norma J. Livo and Dia Cha. We based the story of Jouanah on these sources as well as the oral traditions from Tzexa Cherta Lee's family.

The name by which the Cinderella character is known to the Hmong is Nkauj Nog, pronounced GO-NAH, meaning a young female orphan. In order to make the story more accessible to an American audience, we have chosen the name Ntsuag Nos, pronounced JO-a-nah, meaning a young orphan, either male or female.

Hmong culture is rich and diverse, with a wide variety of clothing decoration and color. For these illustrations, we have elected to show the style of the Blue Hmong clan. Jouanah's skirt is exactly like a skirt purchased in Ban Vinai Camp, Thailand, in 1979. Source materials for other elements include photographs and videos generously provided by the Hmong community of Santa Barbara, California.

n a sun-splashed clearing high in the mountains of the ancient homeland of the Hmong, there lived a farmer, his wife, and their daughter, a kind and beautiful girl, named Jouanah.

"We will never have a good harvest without the help of a cow," fretted the farmer one day. So, he and his wife set off to the market. To their surprise, they found only one cow for sale and already another man was bargaining for it.

Not sure who should get his cow, the owner proposed a contest. He served them bowls of steaming hot rice soup and declared, "Whoever finishes his bowl first will win the right to buy my cow at a very fine price."

The first man slyly slipped cold water into his bowl and quickly drank the soup. The farmer, unaware of the trick, was still blowing his soup when the other man strutted off with the cow.

"We must have a cow to plow our fields and carry the grain," insisted the wife as they walked home. "Let me become a cow for awhile to help bring in the crops. You can care for me and we will all have a good life."

Without a word of protest, the husband took three vines and wound them three times around his wife's ankles, three times around her wrists, and three times around her head.

In a flash of lightning and a clap of thunder, the wife became a cow.

"Father, you bought a cow!" Jouanah ran out to greet him. "Where is Mother? She'll be pleased."

"Jouanah, this cow is your mother."

"What do you mean?" Jouanah asked, puzzled.

"I did what your mother said to do." The father nodded toward the gentle cow standing at his side and told her what had happened.

Shocked at what she heard, Jouanah cried out, "Mother, Mother, please come back!" But the gentle cow, no longer hearing with the ears of a human, simply mooed.

With a heavy heart, Jouanah slowly led the cow toward the far fields.

With the help of the cow, the farm prospered. But then, instead of changing the cow back to his wife, the farmer selfishly married another woman. He told the second wife, who had a daughter near the age of Jouanah, of his duty to care for the cow.

"What is this?" the new wife asked when she heard the husband's story. "Is it not enough that the first wife's daughter is more beautiful than my Ding? Now I am expected to take second place to a cow!"

Worst of all, when she found out that the cow was really Jouanah's mother and was magically spinning rolls of silken thread around her horns for Jouanah, the second wife's heart began to burn within her. She stormed, "Your Jouanah—not my Ding—will cut the wood, cook the meals, and keep this house clean from now on!"

To keep peace, Jouanah and her father worked from dawn till dark. Still, the stepmother and the lazy Ding sulked and grumbled.

"Husband," called the new wife one morning, "my life with you makes me so sick, I am going to die!" And with that, she fell back on her mat, rolled her eyes upward, and groaned loudly. "Go to the giant dead tree at the forest's edge." She clutched her head as if it were throbbing with pain. "Its spirit will tell you how to help me!"

But no sooner had the husband set out than the scheming woman leaped up from her mat and dashed by a shortcut to the old tree. When the man neared the tree, he took three joss sticks of incense and lit them with great reverence. Timidly, he asked the powerful spirit for help.

Pretending to be the tree spirit, the wife disguised her voice and from her hiding place said, "You have a wise wife, my good man. But only one thing will help her. There is an evil spirit in those rolls of thread Jouanah brings home. Burn all the thread and your wife will be healed."

Sadly, the farmer gathered the rolls of shimmering thread and threw them into the cooking fire. They flared into millions of brilliant sparks.

Yet, when roll after roll of secretly spun thread continued to appear in the house each day, the new wife knew she must take even stronger measures.

"Husband," called the wife one morning, "I am so sick, I will not live through the day! Return to the giant dead tree at the forest's edge." She clutched her stomach as if it were throbbing with pain. "Its spirit will tell you how to help me!"

And so again, the farmer went to the tree and asked its powerful spirit for help.

Pretending to be the tree spirit, the wife disguised her voice and from her hiding place said, "You have a wise wife, my good man. But only one thing can save her life. The good spirits of your ancestors demand the sacrifice of a cow. Kill the cow and your wife will not die."

"Kill my cow?" the husband asked mournfully.

On his way home, the husband gasped when he saw the gentle cow already lying lifeless where she had lain down the night before. She had died of a broken heart.

Night after night Jouanah and her father sat on a log near the place where they buried the gentle cow.

It was a very sad time. The birds hushed their songs. The butterflies folded their radiant wings. The despairing husband soon died and the gentle Jouanah fell even more silent. As for the stepmother, she became more and more talkative. She talked about her fine health. She talked about her fine clothes. She talked about her plans for her fine daughter, Ding.

Later, when the New Year arrived, the stepmother and her daughter wanted to be the very first to arrive at the village festivities. Before they set out, the stepmother called to Jouanah. "Girl," she ordered, "see that the rice is clean and ready for dinner." Cruelly, the stepmother had stirred thousands of tiny pebbles into the basket of rice kernels.

Obediently, Jouanah spent the first two days of the New Year celebration picking stones from the rice.

Finally finished on the third day Jouanah sat down to rest. Reaching for her mother's old sewing basket, she pulled out the piece of cowhide she had hidden deep inside. She pressed the soft hair to her cheek and closed her eyes. "Never sit idle, my child," Jouanah remembered her mother saying.

Dutifully, she reached for her sewing, thinking of her mother's promise, "My spirit will always be with you." Suddenly, there in the basket appeared a skirt and a blouse, and an apron embroidered with delicate needlework. Beneath them were a glorious headdress and two exquisite purses bordered with coins that jingled musically when she touched them. And what was that sparkling under the purses? Excitedly, Jouanah uncovered a wondrous silver necklace that shone brilliantly in the late afternoon sun.

Jouanah slipped into the elegant clothes. They fit perfectly. Joyously, she twirled 'round and 'round and the skirt opened wide in a circle of vibrant colors.

She looked into the basket again. There, before her eyes, appeared a pair of dainty shoes. They seemed to dance to the sound of the music drifting from the village. Just then, Jouanah heard her mother's voice. "My daughter, put them on and hurry to the festival!"

Happy, Jouanah tucked the soft cowhide deep into her sewing basket and let her new shoes lead her down the path to the village clearing. She wondered if anyone might recognize her.

"Who is that beautiful girl?" asked the young men at the festival.

"Humph," muttered the stepmother seeing her beauty. But no one knew who the mysterious girl was. Even when Jouanah played catch in the ball-toss game, no one recognized her.

The shadows lengthened. The games were about to end when, at the edge of the clearing a tall, handsome young man appeared. "There is Shee-Nang!" everyone exclaimed, honored to be joined by the son of the village Elder. He was a fine young man of learning and wealth.

Shee-Nang began to play his bamboo instrument. The *qeng* made sweet, stirring sounds. The young man danced gracefully as he played. Jouanah watched, delighted by the music maker. Then their eyes met and the melody encircled her like a tender embrace.

The stepmother wanted the handsome young man to play for her daughter, but Shee-Nang serenaded only the beautiful girl. At this, the stepmother grabbed Ding by the arm and they made off hurriedly toward home.

Jouanah knew that she must arrive home first to have the meal ready. In her haste, she stepped in a muddy puddle, kicked a rock and off came one of her shoes. Jouanah dared not stop, dared not look back. She must rush home.

The handsome Shee-Nang set off after her down the path. "Ah, ha," he exclaimed, when he came upon the dainty shoe. He picked it up and wiped it clean. Then he vowed to himself that nothing would stop him from finding the mysterious, lovely girl whose tiny foot it fit.

From village to village Shee-Nang searched. He searched the farms. He searched the fields. He went from house to house. Everyone heard of his search for the maiden whose shoe he had found.

Eventually he came to Jouanah's house. "This way, kind sir," beckoned the stepmother who had seen Shee-Nang coming. "I recognize that shoe!" Then in a loud whisper, the stepmother called, "Daughter, come!" But to her dismay, both girls appeared at once.

"No, no. Not you." The stepmother tried to wave away the lovely Jouanah.

"Please stay," insisted the young man.

"Don't bother with her," protested the stepmother. Then she pushed her own daughter to the stool directly in front of Shee-Nang. But try as she may, Ding could not put the dainty shoe on her bulging foot.

Shee-Nang then turned to Jouanah. "Please sit here," he said. In a glance, they both could see that the shoe would fit perfectly on her tiny foot. But fearing the stepmother's anger, Jouanah backed away.

The stepmother, her mind still swirling with schemes to trap Shee-Nang for her own daughter, spoke up, "You will do our house honor if you would stay for dinner."

Tired from his long search, Shee-Nang agreed.

The stepmother quickly devised yet another deceitful plan. One dish she would make of tasty rice with meat and the other of dry bones and rice hulls.

Before serving, the stepmother blew out the oil lamps to make the room nearly dark. Then she set the best food before Shee-Nang and Ding while giving the dry bones to Jouanah. She hoped Jouanah would be left so weak from hunger that she could not distract the guest from her daughter.

But the young man saw what the stepmother had done and how sweetly Jouanah had endured the trick. Shee-Nang turned to Jouanah, quietly saying, "We could see better with more light. Where are the other oil lamps?"

Jouanah led Shee-Nang from the table. At the doorway, their eyes met again. No need for words; their hearts touched. The village, they knew, would bless their love. Jouanah swept her mother's sewing basket up into her arms. Then, together, the two young people left for the home of Shee-Nang's parents.

The stepmother and Ding stood in the doorway. Speechless, they watched the couple disappear into the purple shadows of the warm, fragrant night.

After their wedding, Jouanah and Shee-Nang set out for their new life. They made their way past the place where the gentle cow was buried, past the giant dead tree, through the green rice paddy, and across the jungle clearing. At last, they crossed over the wide river to the fertile fields beyond. There, it is said, they lived long, happy lives, turning the sadness Jouanah had known into endless joy.

As far as anyone knows, the stepmother and the lazy Ding are still standing at the door of the house, plotting and scheming, making endless misery for only themselves. The magic piece of soft cowhide is still safely hidden deep in the old sewing basket. Its spirit awaits the fair child of Jouanah and her loving husband. And it will be there even for the child of that child, and the child of that child, and on, and on, and on, as long as this story is told.

The Contributors

Dr. Jewell Reinhart Coburn has lived abroad and studied an array of diverse cultures. She is the recipient of a doctorate in Higher Education Administration and two honorary degrees, plus many literary awards. Her other works for children and young people include *Beyond the East Wind; Encircled Kingdom; Khmers, Tigers and Talismans;* and *Lani and the Secret of the Mountain.*

Tzexa Cherta Lee was the chief editor for *Ntsuag Hlav,* a Hmong newsletter published in Ban Vinai, Thailand. He worked with Fresno Unified Schools in California as a tutor, translator, consultant, and material developer after his arrival in the United States. He is now a doctoral student in Linguistic Anthropology at the University of California, Davis, studying the Hmong language and culture.

Anne Sibley O'Brien grew up in South Korea as the daughter of medical missionaries. She was introduced to the Hmong in 1979 when her parents worked at Ban Vinai refugee camp in Thailand. She has a major in studio art and has illustrated seventeen books for children, including *Talking Walls, Welcoming Babies, Who Belongs Here,* and *The Princess and the Beggar.*

Mai Kou Xiong is a consultant to the Hmong Literacy and Cultural Program for the Lompoc Unified School District in California. She is an effective communicator and is perceived as a role model for Hmong women today in their pursuit of higher education.

Shen's Books publishes books for children and young people that affirm universal values. *Jouanah: A Hmong Cinderella* is available in English, Spanish, and Hmong language editions. A Teacher's Guide is also available:

☎ 800-456-6660